The Adventures of Tom Sawyer

Mark Twain

Simplified by D K Swan
Illustrated by Chris Molan

LONGMAN

Pearson Education Limited,
Edinburgh Gate, Harlow,
Essex CM20 2JE, England
and Associated Companies throughout the world.

This simplified edition © Longman Group UK Limited 1991

First published 1991
This impression Penguin Books 1999

0-582-03588-0

Set in 10/13 point Linotron 202 Versailles
Printed in China
GCC/13

Acknowledgements
The cover background is a wallpaper design called NUAGE,
courtesy of Osborne and Little plc.

Stage 3: 1300 word vocabulary
Please look under *New words* at the back of this book
for explanations of words outside this stage.

Contents

Introduction

Mark Twain

The writer's real name was Samuel Clemens. He was born in 1835 in the state of Missouri, not very far from the little town of Hannibal. Hannibal, on the west bank of the Mississippi River, is the "St Petersburg" of this book. It was then a village (though it is sometimes called a "town" in this book), but it is now a town of about 19,000 people.

Sam's boyhood in Hannibal seems to have been quite happy, though they were rough times in such a place on the edge of civilised America. He was only twelve when his father died, and he had to start work in his older brother's printing works. It was not exciting work for a lover of action, and Sam was glad to change from printing to piloting the Mississippi River steamboats. It was important and difficult work. The water was often not deep enough for a big steamboat, and rain or dry weather farther up the river could make a difference to the speed of the river water as well as to its depth.

Sam Clemens was happy as a river pilot. But the Civil War between North and South (1861–65) put an end to the great days of the river boats. Sam became a newspaper reporter, choosing to write, not as Samuel Clemens, but as "Mark Twain". This was the call of the river-boat leadsman when he tested the depth of the water with his line and found it was two fathoms deep, which enough for a large steamboat (1 fathom=1.83 metres).

It was as a newspaper reporter that Mark Twain joined

a ship taking some of the earliest American tourists to Europe and the East. Out of that came his first full-length book, *The Innocents Abroad* (1869). It was a very funny book, and it showed Americans that they could laugh at themselves. In the book, Mark Twain's tourists visit place after place and judge everything, not for historical or artistic values, but comparing the things seen with things in their own experience. One of their judgements that readers enjoyed was about the great artist Leonardo da Vinci:

> They spell it Vinci and pronounce it Vinchy; foreigners always spell better than they pronounce.

The success of that book made it possible for Mark Twain to end his work as a newspaper reporter, and spend his time writing books. His two most famous books are this one: *The Adventures of Tom Sawyer* (1876), and – much later, in 1884 – *The Adventures of Huckleberry Finn*. The setting for both is the great Mississippi River that had meant so much to Samuel Clemens as a boy and as a young man.

The Mississippi River

The name Mississippi means "Father of waters" in the Algonquin Indian language. The river, 3,779 kilometres long, begins at a height of 446 metres in the state of Minnesota. It flows at first between high cliff-like banks, then through valleys which are thickly forested. It receives water from a number of other rivers, including the Illinois and America's longest river, the Missouri. These rivers formed the way for the settlement of the central United States. When steamboats arrived, from 1812, there was a great increase in travel and trade.

A place like Hannibal (Mark Twain's "St Petersburg") would be visited by steamboats carrying passengers or goods up or down the river. The people would also see great rafts of logs from the forests on the banks. Several men would live on these rafts, taking them down the river to the sawmills at the ports.

The river, then, was very important in the life of a place like Hannibal. And that is why, in play, a boy like Ben Rogers "was the *Big Missouri*, a great river steamboat nearly three metres deep in the water. He was the steamboat, and the captain, and the engine-room bells."

The Cave

There is a cave south of Hannibal that is very much like the "McDougal's Cave" of this story. The real cave, McDowell's Cave, is visited every year by thousands of tourists. They don't use candles now, and they don't get lost. They visit it because it has real wonders – rather like the "Hall", the "Great Church", "Aladdin's Palace" and other wonders of "McDougal's Cave" – but mainly they go because it is important in a favourite book: *The Adventures of Tom Sawyer*.

Chapter 1
Tom misses school

"Tom!"

No answer.

"Tom!"

No answer.

"Where *is* that boy? You Tom!"

The old lady went to the open door and stood there, looking out into the garden. She couldn't see Tom, so she shouted, "You-u-u— Tom!"

There was a very small sound behind her, and she turned just in time to catch a small boy by the back of his shirt. "Ah!" she said. "I ought to have remembered that cupboard. What were you doing in there?"

"Nothing."

"Nothing? Look at your hands, and look at your mouth. What *is* that red stuff?"

"*I* don't know, Aunt."

"Well, *I* know. It's jam. That's what it is. I've told you forty times, if you steal that jam I'll take your skin off. Pass me that little stick."

The stick was in the air, ready to bring down punishment.

"Oh! Look behind you, Aunt!"

The old lady turned quickly and gathered her long skirt out of danger. The boy quickly ran out, climbed up the garden fence, and disappeared over it. His Aunt Polly stood for a moment, surprised, and then laughed quietly.

"That boy! Can't I ever learn? He's played that sort of trick often enough, so I ought to be ready. But the trick's always different. And he seems to know just how far he can go before I get angry. And he knows that if he makes me laugh, I can't punish him. I ought to punish him much more often than I do, but he's my poor dead sister's boy. Every time I hit him my heart nearly breaks. He'll miss school this afternoon, I know. I'll have to make him work tomorrow – Saturday – as a punishment. I don't like making him work on a Saturday, but he hates work, and I've got to do my duty in one way or another. If I don't, it'll spoil him."

Tom did miss school, and he had a very good time.

At supper, Aunt Polly asked him a question.

"I expect it was hot in school, wasn't it?" she said.

"Yes, Aunt."

"Didn't you want to have a swim, Tom?"

"She knows something," Tom thought. He studied her face, but it told him nothing. So he said, "No, Aunt – well, not very much."

The old lady reached out and felt Tom's shirt. She said, "But you aren't too hot now."

She thought that was a clever way to discover that Tom's shirt was dry. But Tom guessed her purpose, and he knew what she would try next. He said, "Some of us put our heads under the water pipe on the way home to get cool. My hair's still wet, as you can feel."

Aunt Polly knew he had beaten her. But she thought of something else: "If you just put your head under the pipe, you didn't need to undo your shirt where I sewed it up at the neck. Let me see."

Tom showed her. His shirt was certainly sewed up at the neck.

"Oh!" his aunt said. "I was sure you had missed school and gone swimming. I'm glad I was wrong."

They had both forgotten that Sidney was there. Sidney

was Tom's half-brother, a quiet boy who was never in trouble, but who liked to see Tom in trouble.

"Well," said Sidney, "I thought you sewed his shirt up with white thread, not black."

"Oh!" said Aunt Polly. "Yes, I did sew it with white thread. Tom!"

But Tom hadn't waited. As he went out of the door, he said, "Sid, I'll half kill you for that."

Tom's evening amusements included a fight that tore and dirtied his clothes although he won the fight. He got home rather late, and when he climbed through the window his aunt was waiting for him. She saw the condition of his clothes, and she knew that she must make him work on Saturday morning.

Chapter 2
Saturday morning

It was Saturday morning and the summer world was bright.

Tom came out of the gate with a bucket of white paint and a long brush. He looked at the fence, and the joy left his heart. Thirty metres of fence, three metres high! He shook his head as he painted the top board at one end, and then looked at the great length of unpainted fence. He began to think of the fun he had planned for the day. Soon the free boys would come past him on their way to all sorts of fun. They would laugh at him because he had to work. He thought of the things in his pockets: a fishing line, a few pieces of string, one or two broken toys, a bone – enough, perhaps, to buy a few minutes' change of work, but not enough to buy even half an hour of freedom. He put the things back in his pockets. And then – at this dark and hopeless moment – the great idea came to him. He took his brush and began calmly to paint.

Ben Rogers came in sight – the one boy whose laughter he had feared. Ben was eating an apple and making noises that showed he was the *Big Missouri*, a great river steamboat nearly three metres deep in the water. He was the steamboat, and the captain, and the engine-room bells. As he came near to Tom, he slowed down, leaned far over to the right, and moved in towards the sidewalk. "Stop her! Ling-a-ling-ling!" The great wheels turned slowly through the water, one side after the other, until the captain had brought his ship close to where Tom was painting. Tom didn't stop. He paid no attention to the steamboat. He looked with an artist's eye at the work he had done. Then he touched it in a few places with his brush.

"Hullo!" Ben said. "You've got to work, have you?"

"Oh, hullo! It's you, Ben. I didn't notice you."

"I'm going swimming," Ben said. "Don't you want to swim? But perhaps you'd rather work!"

Tom stopped for a moment and looked at him. "Work? What do you call work?"

"Isn't that work?"

Tom stopped painting again. He answered carelessly, "Well, perhaps it is, and perhaps it isn't. All I know is, it's all right for Tom Sawyer."

"You don't really pretend you like it?"

The brush continued to move. "Like it? Well, of course I like it. A boy doesn't get a chance to paint a fence every day." Tom gave a few more touches of his brush, and then stepped back to look at his work – added a little paint – put his head on one side, and looked again.

"Say, Tom, let me paint a little."

Tom thought. "No," he said. "I can't let you. Aunt Polly's very proud of this fence – her front fence on the street. It's got to be done very carefully. Very few boys can paint it the way it must be done."

"Is that so? But let me just try. I'll be very careful. I – I'll give you my apple."

Tom gave him the brush – with doubt on his face, but joy in his heart.

The *Big Missouri* steamboat changed into an artist, and worked hard under the hot sun, while Tom lay in the shade. He ate his apple, and planned his future victories. There were plenty of these. Boys came along the street, stopped to make fun of the workers – and stayed to try to be artists. By the time Ben was tired, Tom had sold the next chance to Billy Fisher for an arrow in quite good condition. When Billy couldn't do any more, Johnny Miller bought the next chance for a dead rat and a string to swing it with. And so it went on, hour after hour. By the middle of the afternoon, Tom was rich. Besides the things I have named, he had twelve marbles, part of a drum, a piece of blue bottle-glass to look through, a key that wouldn't unlock anything, a bit of red chalk, a tin soldier, a frog, six fireworks, part of a door knocker, a knife without a point, four pieces of orange skin, and an old window lock. He had had a nice lazy time in the shade, with plenty of company, and the fence had three coats of white paint on it.

Tom went to find Aunt Polly.

"May I go and play now, Aunt?" he asked.

"What! Already? How much have you done?"

"It's all done, Aunt."

"Tom, don't tell me lies. I can't bear it."

"It's not lies, Aunt. It *is* all done."

Aunt Polly went to see for herself. She expected to see about one-fifth of the fence done. She found the whole fence painted, and even some of the ground in front of the fence. She was so surprised that she went to the cupboard, chose a big apple, and gave it to Tom. While she was choosing it, Tom "won" a tea cake from a plate in the cupboard.

As Tom was going to join his friends, he passed Judge Thatcher's house. There was a new girl in the garden – a lovely little girl with yellow hair. Tom had thought he was in love with Amy Lawrence, but Amy disappeared from his heart. Her place was taken by the girl with yellow hair.

Another boy paints the fence, while Tom rests

Chapter 3
School

Monday morning came, and Tom Sawyer was miserable. He was always miserable on Monday morning because it began another week's slow suffering in school.

Tom lay thinking. He thought that if he were sick, he could stay at home and not go to school. He gave his attention to his body. He couldn't find any illness. For a moment he thought he felt a stomachache, but it disappeared. He tried again. Suddenly he discovered something: one of his upper teeth was loose. He groaned.

His groan failed to wake Sid up.

Tom groaned louder, and even imagined that he felt the tooth ache. But Sid didn't move.

"Sid! Sid!" And Tom began to groan again.

Sid moved, stretched, and then sat up suddenly as Tom's groaning grew louder.

"Tom! What's the matter, Tom?"

"I forgive you for everything, Sid. [*Groan*] Everything you've ever done to me. When I'm gone——"

"Oh, Tom, you aren't dying, are you? Don't, Tom. Oh, don't!"

"I forgive everybody, Sid. [*Groan*] Tell them, Sid——"

But Sid had gone. By this time Tom's imagination was working so well that he was really suffering, and his groans sounded real.

Sid ran downstairs and said, "Oh, Aunt Polly, come! Tom's dying!"

"Dying? I don't believe it!"

But she ran upstairs, with Sid following her.

"You Tom!" she cried. "Tom, what's the matter?"

"It's my tooth, Auntie. It's dying."

The old lady sat down in a chair, and laughed a little, and cried a little, and then did both together. That made her feel better, so she said, "What's the matter with your tooth?"

"One of them's loose, and it aches terribly."

"Open your mouth. Hm! Well, your tooth *is* loose, but you're not going to die. Sid, get me a length of silk thread and a piece of burning wood from the kitchen fire."

Tom said, "Oh, please, Auntie, don't pull it out. It's stopped hurting. Truly it's better. I don't want to stay at home instead of going to school."

"Ah! Now I understand. You thought you'd stay away from school and go fishing? Tom, Tom, I love you so much, and you seem to try every way to break my old heart by your terrible tricks."

By this time, Sid had brought the thread and fire. The old lady tied one end of the thread to Tom's tooth, and the other end to the bedpost. Then she took the burning wood and suddenly moved it almost into Tom's face. The result was that the tooth hung from the bedpost.

But there is a good side to most suffering. The gap in Tom's front teeth made it possible for him to spit in a new and wonderful way, so all the other boys wished they had a gap like it.

On his way to school, Tom met Huckleberry Finn. Huckleberry was the son of the town's drunkard – its hard-drinking bad man. All the mothers of the town hated and feared Huckleberry because he was lazy, and lawless, and without manners, and bad – and because their children thought he was wonderful. Tom was like the other boys: he wished he could be like Huckleberry, and he was forbidden to play with him. So he played with him whenever he had a chance. Huckleberry always wore grown men's thrown-away clothes. He slept on doorsteps in fine weather and in empty barrels in wet weather. Nobody made him go to school or to church. He could go fishing or swimming when and where he pleased. Nobody told him not to fight. He was always the first boy to go without shoes in the spring. He never had to wash or put on clean clothes. He could swear wonderfully. He had everything that makes life precious, as every well cared for, properly behaved boy in St Petersburg could see.

The meeting resulted in a conversation about Tom's tooth and a dead cat that Huckleberry had found. And so Tom was late in reaching the school.

"Thomas Sawyer!" said the master.

Tom knew that when any grown-up said his full name it meant trouble.

"Thomas Sawyer, come here! Now, why are you late again, as usual?"

Tom was just going to tell a lie when he saw the yellow hair hanging down a back – a back that he knew by the electric power of love. And he saw that the only empty place on the girls' side of the schoolroom was beside the owner of the hair. He looked straight at the master and said, "I STOPPED TO TALK TO HUCKLEBERRY FINN!"

The master's heart stopped, and he looked helpless. The other students wondered, "Has Tom gone mad?"

The master said, "Tom – you did what?"

"Stopped to talk to Huckleberry Finn."

"Thomas Sawyer, this is the most terrible thing I have heard. Prepare yourself for punishment!"

The master's arm worked until it was tired and there were no more thin sticks. Then came the order that everybody expected: "Now, go and sit with the *girls*!"

Tom's face went rather red, but that was not because the other children laughed, but because he felt so lucky as he sat down beside the girl with yellow hair.

After a time, he looked at the girl, but she turned her back towards him. When she turned round again, there was an apple in front of her. She pushed it away. Tom gently put it back, and she pushed it away again – but less angrily. Tom wrote, "Please take it. Got more." She looked at the words, but did nothing. Tom began to draw some-thing, hiding the drawing with his left hand. For a time, the girl pretended not to notice, but her natural curiosity began to show itself. The boy worked on. At last she whispered, "Let me see it."

Tom partly uncovered a very bad drawing of a house.

"It's nice," she said. "Make a man."

The artist added a man in front of the house. It was a very big man who could have stepped over the house, but the girl liked it. "It's a beautiful man," she said. "Now make me coming along."

Tom drew a moon with arms and legs.

The girl said, "It's lovely! I wish I could draw."

"It's easy," Tom whispered. "I'll teach you. What's your name?"

"Becky Thatcher. What's yours? – oh, I know. It's Tho-mas Sawyer."

"That's the name they beat me by. I'm Tom when I'm good. You'll call me Tom, will you?"

"Yes."

At this moment, the boy felt strong fingers close on his ear and begin to lift him. The hold on his ear took him painfully across the room and dropped him in his own seat while the other children laughed.

Tom's ear hurt, but his heart was full of joy.

Chapter 4
Huckleberry Finn

Tom waited after morning school, but the girl didn't speak to him. He decided to miss afternoon school to show her that he didn't care.

He walked through the trees, thinking of ways to make her value his friendship.

He would be a soldier, and return after many years, war-worn and famous.

No. Better than that, he would join the Indians and go hunting, and lead his men on the warpath over the mountains to the great plains of the Far West. Then, far in the future, he would come back, a great chief with painted face and huge feathered headdress. He would rush into Sunday school one fine summer morning, putting fear into the hearts of his friends with his loud war whoops.

But no. There was something greater. He would be a pirate! That was it! His name would fill the world, and make people shake with fear. How fearlessly he would sail over the oceans in his fast ship, the *Spirit of the Storm*, with the black pirate flag flying. And, when his name was most famous, he would come back to the old town. People would see his weather-beaten face, his fine clothes, the hand guns and crime-marked sword. He would hear them whispering, "It's Tom Sawyer the Pirate! The Black Avenger of the Spanish Main!"

It was just then that the sound of a toy trumpet came through the forest. Tom quickly took off his jacket and trousers. He pulled some plants aside and took from their hiding place a roughly made bow and arrow, a wooden sword and a toy trumpet. With these things he ran through the forest until he reached a certain big tree. There he stopped and blew an answering call on his "horn", and then began to move slowly forward, looking to right and left.

"Wait here, my merry men!" he said to an imaginary company. "Stay hidden until I blow."

Joe Harper appeared, also in only his long shirt and with bow and arrow and sword.

"Ho!" called Tom. "Who comes into Sherwood Forest without my pass?"

"Guy of Gisborne needs no man's pass. Who are you?"

"Robin Hood."

"Well, then, if you are the famous Robin Hood, draw your sword!"

The sword fight went on until Tom shouted, "Fall down! Why don't you fall?"

"Why don't you fall yourself?"

"Because that isn't in the book. The book says, 'Then with one fierce swing to the neck, Robin killed the luckless Guy of Gisborne.' You must turn round and let me hit the back of your neck."

There was no arguing with "the book" (as remembered by Tom). So Joe turned, received the hit, and fell.

"Now," said Joe, getting up, "you've got to let me kill you. That's fair."

"But I can't do that. It isn't in the book."

"Well, it isn't fair."

"Well, all right, Joe. You can be Friar Tuck, or Much the Miller's Son, and hit me with your quarterstaff. Or I'll be the Sheriff of Nottingham, and you be Robin Hood for a time, and kill me."

This was "fair". So these adventures were carried out.

Then the boys dressed themselves for the modern world, hid their Sherwood Forest things, and went towards their homes.

After Tom had said goodbye to Joe, he met Huckleberry Finn carrying the dead cat.

"What's the cat for, Huck?" Tom asked.

"Cure warts."

"How do you cure warts with a dead cat?"

"You wait until somebody bad has been buried. When it's midnight, a devil will come – or two or three – to the grave to take the bad man's body away. You can't see the devils; you just hear something like the wind, or you hear them talking. Then when they're taking the body away, you throw your cat after them, and you have to say: 'Devil follow body; cat follow devil; warts follow cat. *I've* finished with *you*!' That'll take *any* wart away."

Tom agreed. It sounded right.

"When are you going to do it, Huck?" he asked.

"Tonight. They buried Horse Williams today. I'm going to be in the graveyard just before midnight. Are you coming? The devils are sure to come."

Chapter 5
Murder

Tom and Huckleberry Finn waited in silence for a long time near the new grave in the graveyard.

At last Tom had to say something. He whispered:

"Hucky, do you believe the dead people like us to be here?"

Huckleberry thought for a moment.

"I wish I knew," he whispered.

"Hucky, do you suppose Horse Williams can hear us talking?"

"Of course he can. Or his spirit can."

Another silence.

"I wish I'd said *Mister* Williams. But everybody called him Horse."

"You can't be too careful what you say about these dead people," said Huckleberry.

There was no more talk after that until Tom suddenly caught hold of his friend's arm and said:

"*Sh!* Listen!"

The boys almost stopped breathing. From the far side of the graveyard came a sound of voices. Then a lamp was seen as the voices came nearer.

"I never knew devils needed a lamp," said Tom.

"*Sh!*"

"What's happening, Huck?"

"They aren't devils. They're people. Well, one of them is. One of the voices is old Muff Potter's. I know it. Don't move. He won't see us. He'll be drunk as usual."

"All right, Huck. I won't move. Look. They've stopped. They can't find it. – They're coming this way now. And

15

Huck, I know another of their voices: it's Injun Joe!"

"You're right. It's that murdering thief. I'd rather it *was* a devil."

The boys couldn't say anything more. The three men had reached the grave.

"Here it is," said the third voice. And the lamp showed the face of young Dr Robinson. "Hurry, men! The moon may come out soon."

For some time there was no sound except the noises of digging. The moon came out from behind clouds as Potter and Injun Joe dug up the body, rolled it in cloth of some kind, and tied the top and bottom with rope. Potter took out a big knife and cut off the ends of the rope. Then he said, "Now it's ready for you, doctor. And you'll give us five more dollars."

"That's right," said Injun Joe.

"What do you mean?" said the doctor. "You asked for your money before we started, and I gave you the amount we agreed."

"Yes," said Injun Joe. "But you owe me more. Perhaps you've forgotten, but I haven't. Five years ago I came to your father's kitchen to ask for some food. You said I had come to steal something, and you and your father had me put in prison. Did you think I could forget? I've got you now, and you'll have to pay."

He stepped close to the young doctor with his arm raised. The doctor suddenly hit out, and Injun Joe fell to the ground. Potter dropped his knife and took hold of the doctor, crying, "Don't you hit my friend!"

The two men struggled, each trying to throw the other down. Injun Joe jumped up, his eyes full of hate. He picked up Potter's knife and moved like a cat round the fighting men, looking for a chance to use the knife.

16

Suddenly the doctor freed himself, took up the board that had marked Williams's grave, and used it to strike Potter to the ground. And at the same moment, Injun Joe saw his chance and drove the knife into the young man. The doctor fell, partly on Potter, pouring blood over him.

Just then, clouds covered the moon again, and the two frightened boys went running as fast as they could through the dark.

Injun Joe made sure the doctor was dead. Then he stole everything he could find on the body. He put the knife into Potter's right hand, then sat down and waited.

Three – four – five minutes passed, and then Potter groaned. He opened his eyes, saw the body, saw the knife in his own hand. "I – I didn't do it!" he said.

"You did," said Joe.

The two boys ran towards the village. From time to time they looked back over their shoulders. Every bush and tree seemed to be coming after them.

At last they reached the old storehouse, ran inside, and felt safer in the shadows beyond the door.

After a time their breathing was easier, and Tom whispered, "Huck, what do you think'll happen?"

"If Dr Robinson dies, they'll hang someone."

"Who'll tell? Will we?"

"What are you talking about, Tom? Suppose for some reason Injun Joe didn't get hung, then he'd kill *us* some time. You can be sure of that."

"That's just what I was thinking, Huck."

"Tom, we've got to keep mum about this. That Injun Joe would kill us without a moment's thought if we told and if they didn't hang him. We must swear to say nothing. That's what we must do – swear to keep mum."

Tom and Huck see the murder in the graveyard

"You're right, Huck. That's the best thing. Shall we just hold hands and swear that we——"

"Oh, no. That's not enough for this. There has to be writing about a big thing like this. And blood!"

Tom agreed with all his heart. It was deep and dark, and fearful. He picked up a piece of board that lay near the door, took the piece of red chalk from his pocket, got the moonlight on his work, and carefully wrote these lines:

> *Huck Finn and Tom Sawyer swear they will Keep Mum about this and they wish they may Drop Down Dead if they ever tell.*

Huckleberry thought Tom was very clever to write so well. Tom took the thread from a needle he kept in his jacket, and he got enough blood from a finger to write "TS" on the board. Then he helped Huckleberry Finn to make his "HF", and the work was done. They hid the board under the floor in a dark corner.

Chapter 6
Jackson's Island

The news of the murder spread through the village very quickly. By midday everybody knew about it, and that a bloody knife lying near the dead man belonged to Muff Potter. And before long, Potter was caught and locked up.

Tom was very worried. Muff Potter was in the village lock-up, and they would probably hang him for a murder he hadn't done. Injun Joe was still around, and a danger to the two boys. But there was another trouble: Becky Thatcher was sick. Tom thought she might die. He lost interest in war, and even in pirates.

His aunt tried all sorts of medicines to cure his loss of interest in life. Every day she filled him up with cures, but Tom was still miserable.

It was then that she heard of Pain-killer. She bought a lot and tasted it. It was liquid fire, so she was sure it must be good. She gave Tom a small spoonful. He asked for some more, and she was delighted.

The truth was that Tom was rather tired of dying for love. He decided to pretend to like Pain-killer. He asked for it so often that in the end she gave him the bottle and told him to take as much as he liked.

Because it was Tom, she watched the bottle. She saw that the amount of Pain-killer in it really did become less. She didn't know that he was using it to cure a small opening in the sitting room floor.

One day Tom was curing the hole in the floor when his aunt's yellow cat Peter came along. Peter looked at the spoon with interest and showed that he wanted a taste.

"Don't ask for it unless you want it, Peter," said Tom.

Peter showed that he did want it.

"Are you quite sure?"

Peter was sure.

So Tom opened Peter's mouth and poured down the Pain-killer. Peter sprang two metres into the air, gave a loud war whoop, and set off round and round the room, crashing against the furniture, knocking over the flower pots, and generally shaking up the room. Next he rose on his back legs and danced round in a mad spin of pleasure, his voice telling the world how happy he was. Then he raced round the house again, spreading disorder everywhere. Aunt Polly came in just in time to see him jump several times for joy, give a last loud cheer, and fly through the open window, carrying the rest of the flower pots with him. The old lady stood turned to stone in her surprise. Tom was lying on the floor, dying with laughter.

"Tom! What *is* the matter with that cat?"

Tom stopped laughing for long enough to say, "*I* don't know, Aunt."

"But I've never seen anything like it. What *did* make him behave like that?"

"Indeed I don't know, Aunt Polly. Cats always behave like that when they're enjoying themselves."

"They do, do they?" Something in her voice warned Tom of trouble.

The old lady was looking down. Too late, Tom saw the handle of the spoon showing under the bed cover. Aunt Polly picked it up. Then she raised Tom by the usual handle – his ear – and hit his head with the spoon.

Tom went out into an unkind world. When he met his friend Joe Harper, he wanted to tell him all about the unkindness of his home and the world outside. But he

Peter jumps through the open window

found that Joe Harper wanted to tell *him* of the unkindness of *his* world. His mother had punished him for drinking some cream, although he hadn't done it. He hoped she wouldn't be sorry for sending him out to suffer in a cruel world.

Joe thought he would find a cave in a far-away desert and live on pieces of old bread until he died quite soon. But Tom showed him that a life of crime would be much better. So the two boys decided to be pirates.

Five kilometres down river from St Petersburg, at a point where the Mississippi River was just over one and a half kilometres wide, there was a long, narrow, tree-covered island – Jackson's Island. It seemed a good place for pirates to meet. Nobody lived there. It was near to the other side of the river – the Illinois side – where there was thick forest and there were hardly any people. They didn't wonder who they would attack as pirates.

Then they looked for and found Huckleberry Finn, and he was glad to join them. They separated after agreeing to meet at midnight at a place on the river bank. Each of them would bring fishing hooks and lines and any food that he could steal in the most secret and mysterious piratical way.

At about midnight, Tom arrived with some cold cooked meat and other things. He stopped near the river bank in some thick bushes and listened. There was no sound. The great river lay like a sleeping ocean. Tom gave a low whistle. An answering whistle came from the river bank. Then a voice asked, "Who's there?"

"Tom Sawyer, the Black Avenger of the Spanish Main. What are your names?"

"Huck Finn the Red-handed, and Joe Harper the Terror of the Seas." Tom had found the names in one of his favourite books.

"Give the password," the Black Avenger said.

Two piratical whispers gave the awful word: "BLOOD!"

The Terror of the Seas had brought bread and beans. Finn the Red-handed had "found" a pan, and a few other kitchen things. None of them had any fire – matches were hardly known in that part of the country – so they went up the bank to where they saw a fire on a great raft tied to the shore. The raft men were all down at the village, but the boys made a great adventure of stealing some burning wood. They carried it to a smaller raft of only a few logs that did not seem to belong to anybody. And then they set off.

At two o'clock in the morning, they brought the raft to the head of Jackson's Island. They landed their stores, made a fire about ten metres inside the forest edge, and cooked supper.

After a time, Huck said in a rather sleepy voice, "What do pirates have to do?"

"Oh, they just have a good time. They take ships, and burn them, and get the money, and bury it in secret places. They kill everybody in the ships——"

"Except the women," said Joe. "They carry the women to their island."

"Why?" asked Huck.

"I don't know," said Tom, "but heroes never kill women." He was sleepy too, and soon all three boys were asleep.

Chapter 7
Tom is thought to be dead

The morning began well. The pirates had a swim and caught fish for breakfast. Then they explored the other parts of the island. Jackson's Island was about five kilometres long and less than half a kilometre wide. The thick forest had some pleasant open spaces between the trees, with grass and even flowers.

They took a swim about once an hour, so it was the afternoon before they got back to their camp fire. Their raft had been carried away by the river during the night, but it didn't seem to matter.

After a time, they heard a sound in the distance.

"Like a gun," said Joe.

They ran to the bank nearest to St Petersburg and looked out from behind bushes. There were a lot of boats on the river, and the little St Petersburg steamboat was in the middle of the river not far below the village. There were a lot of people on her. While the boys were looking, a cloud of white smoke came from the side of the steamboat. Moments later, they heard the sound of the distant gun again.

"Oh! I know now," said Tom. "Somebody's drowned."

"That's it!" Huck agreed. "They did that last summer when Bill Turner got drowned. They shoot a big gun over the water, and that makes him come up to the top. I wonder who it is."

The gun had fired twice more when Tom said, "Hey! I know who's drowned. It's us!"

At once they felt like heroes. People had missed them. People were weeping and remembering how unkind they

The boys watch the steamboat from the island

had been to the poor lost boys. The whole village was talking about them.

They caught fish and had supper. Huck was the first to fall asleep, and Joe soon followed. Tom watched them in the light of the camp fire. Then he chose two thin white pieces of "paper" from the bark of a young sycamore tree. He wrote something on each with his piece of red chalk. He put one of these messages in his jacket pocket, and the other in Joe's hat. He also put into the hat certain things of great value: a piece of white chalk, a special ball, three fish hooks, and a marble of the kind known as "sure winner". Then he went silently away to the bank of the island nearest to the Illinois shore.

The water wasn't deep until he was about a hundred metres from the Illinois bank, and then he had to swim. The river carried him down faster than he had expected, but at last he climbed out. He felt in his pocket: his second message was safe. Then he started to walk, with the water pouring from his clothes.

Just before ten o'clock, he was at the steamboat's landing place on the side of the river opposite St Petersburg. The steamboat was there, ready to make its last crossing for the night. Tom slipped quietly down the bank and swam to the small boat that the steamboat always pulled behind it. He hid in the bottom of the small boat.

After the fifteen minutes' crossing to St Petersburg, he swam to the bank about fifty metres down river so as to avoid meeting any passengers. Then he ran by dark footpaths until he reached his aunt's back fence and climbed over it.

A light was burning in the sitting room. Tom looked through the window. Aunt Polly, Sid, Tom's sister Mary, and Joe Harper's mother were sitting together, talking.

27

The bed was between them and the door, so Tom went to the door and opened it very slowly and carefully.

"Why is the candle blowing like that?" said Aunt Polly. "I think the door's open. Go and shut it, Sid."

Tom disappeared under the bed just in time. He lay and took deep breaths for a minute, and then he moved nearer to where he could see his aunt's foot.

"But as I was saying," said Aunt Polly, "he wasn't *bad* – not really – just loved fun. He never meant any harm. Indeed he was the best-hearted, most well-meaning boy" —— and she began to cry.

"My Joe was like that too – couldn't keep out of trouble – but he was always kind. And I punished him for taking that cream. I forgot I had thrown it out because it was bad. And now I'll never, never see him again, the poor, poor boy!" And Mrs Harper cried as if her heart would break.

"I hope Tom's in a happier world," said Sid, "but if he'd been a better boy——"

"*Sid*!" Tom couldn't see the angry look in the old lady's eye, but he could almost feel it. "Not a word against my Tom! He's gone, and I won't hear a word against him from *you*. Oh, Mrs Harper, I don't know how to live without him. He was such a comfort to me, although he made a terrible lot of trouble for me."

"Yes," said Joe's mother. "It's hard – very hard. Only last Saturday my Joe exploded a firecracker almost under my nose, and I knocked him down. I didn't know then how soon – oh, if it happened now, I'd bless him for it."

"Yes, yes, I know just how you feel, Mrs Harper. Only yesterday, my Tom filled the cat full of Pain-killer and I thought the cat was going to tear the house down. I hit Tom with the medicine spoon, poor boy, poor dead boy."

Tom nearly came out from under the bed to comfort his aunt, but he lay still. He went on listening, and he slowly understood what had happened from things that were said. At first people thought the boys had gone for a swim and had drowned. Then the small raft was missed (it did belong to somebody) and everybody expected the boys to land at the next town down river. But then the raft was found on the Missouri shore nine or ten kilometres below the village, and everybody lost hope. If nobody found the bodies before the church service on Sunday, the minister was going to speak about the poor dead boys.

Mrs Harper and Aunt Polly had a good cry together before Joe's mother went home. Tom had to stay under the bed until his aunt was asleep before he could move. He was going to put his sycamore bark "letter" beside the bed, but he had another idea, and he put it back in his pocket. Very gently he kissed his aunt before he left the house. He took the steamboat's small boat and rowed it to the other side. He left it there and went back to the island by walking and swimming. The sun was quite high in the sky by the time he arrived at the pirates' camp fire. There he heard Joe say, "No, Huck. He'll come back. He's too proud to leave us. He's got an idea – that's what it is. One of his ideas! I wonder what he's doing."

"Well, the things are ours, aren't they?"

"Not yet, Huck. The writing says they're ours if he doesn't get back for breakfast."

"And that's what he *has* done!" cried Tom, enjoying the surprise as he stepped into camp.

Tom told all his adventures – with some additions – and then he slept while the other pirates fished and explored.

Chapter 8
Tom returns

On Sunday the people of St Petersburg went to church to hear the minister speak about the poor lost boys whose death had brought such sorrow to the village.

As the people came out of church, there in a line stood the three boys, wet but alive. They had crossed to the Missouri shore, using a log as a boat, and they had landed about eight kilometres below the village. It was Tom's idea to arrive at the church for the service that he had heard about when he was under the bed.

Aunt Polly, Mary and the Harpers threw themselves on their loved ones with kisses and other shows of joy. Huck stood alone, looking and feeling unwanted. He was going to slip away, but Tom caught his arm and said, "Aunt Polly, it isn't fair. Somebody's got to be glad to see Huck."

"And so they will! I'm glad to see him, poor mother-less thing!" And she was so kind and loving to him that he felt even more uncomfortable than before.

It was at breakfast the next day that Aunt Polly said, "Don't you think, Tom, that you could have let me know earlier that you were alive and well?"

"I'm sure he would have done if he had thought of it," Mary said.

"I wish I had thought," said Tom, "but at least I did dream about you."

"Did you, Tom?" Aunt Polly sounded much happier. "What did you dream?"

"It was Wednesday night. I dreamt you were sitting

over there by the bed, and Sid was sitting by the wood box, and Mary next to him."

"Yes. That's what we always do."

"And I dreamt that Joe Harper's mother was here."

"Yes! She was here! Did you dream any more?"

"Oh, lots. But it isn't very clear now."

"Try to remember, won't you?"

"Well, it seems to me that the wind – the wind blew the – the – "

"Do try harder, Tom! The wind did blow something. What?"

Tom pressed his fingers to his head for a minute. Then he said, "Ah! Now I remember! It blew the candle!"

"My word! Go on, Tom, go on!"

"And it seems to me that you said you thought the door was open. You told Sid to go and – and –"

"Yes," said Aunt Polly. "Go on, Tom. What did I tell him to do in your dream?"

"I think you made him shut it."

"Well! That proves it! Don't tell me dreams don't mean anything. Go on, Tom."

"Oh, it's getting clearer now. You said I wasn't really bad, just fun-loving. And then you began to cry."

"So I did. So I did. And then——"

"Then Mrs Harper began to cry, and she said Joe was the same, and she wished she hadn't punished him for taking the cream that she had thrown out herself."

"Tom! This is wonderful! – Go on, Tom!"

"Then Sid said – he said –"

"I don't think I said anything," said Sid.

"Yes, you did, Sid," said Mary.

"Be quiet and let Tom go on. What did he say, Tom?"

"He said – I think he said he hoped I was in a happier

world, but if I'd been better sometimes——"

"There! D'you hear that? His very own words!"

"And you stopped him sharply."

"I certainly did!"

"And Mrs Harper told about Joe frightening her with a firecracker, and you told about Peter and the Pain-killer ——"

"Just as true as I'm alive!"

"And then there was a lot more talk about what happened, and about the arrangements for Sunday, and——"

"Wonderful!" said Aunt Polly. "Oh! But look at the time. You'll have to run to school, all of you."

Only Sid thought – but didn't say what he thought: "As long a dream as that, without any mistakes in it!"

Tom arrived home from school to find an angry Aunt Polly waiting for him.

"Tom! Why don't I take the skin off you?"

"Why? What have I done, Auntie?"

"You've done enough! I go over to see Mrs Harper, and I expect to make her believe all that stuff about your dream. But she had found out from Joe that you were here that night and heard all our talk. How could you come here all the way from Jackson's Island to laugh at our troubles? You never thought about having pity for us and saving us from sorrow."

"Auntie, I know now it was wrong, but I didn't come here to laugh at you that night."

"What did you come for, then?"

"It was to tell you not to worry about us because we weren't drowned."

"Then why – oh, why didn't you do it, Tom?"

"Well, you see, Auntie, when you talked about the

church service, I just got full of the idea of the church service for us, and of coming to the service for a surprise. It seemed such a good idea that I just put the letter back in my pocket and kept mum."

"What letter?"

"The piece of sycamore bark. I had put on it: 'We aren't dead – we've only gone to be pirates' in chalk. I wish now – I wish you'd woken up when I kissed you."

The aunt's face became more gentle. "*Did* you kiss me, Tom?"

"Yes, Auntie."

"Well, kiss me again – and hurry away to school."

As soon as he had gone, she ran to a cupboard and got out the hard-worn jacket that he had used for his pirating adventure. Then she stopped, with the jacket in her hand, and said to herself, "No! I daren't. Poor boy, he's probably told me a lie. And it's a very comforting lie. But I don't want to know it's a lie. I won't look."

She put the jacket away. Twice she put out her hand to take it again – and stopped. At last she did put her hand in the jacket pocket. And a moment later she was reading Tom's piece of bark, with tears pouring down her face.

"I could forgive the boy now if he'd been bad a million times!"

Chapter 9
Becky Thatcher

The one thing Mr Dobbins, the schoolmaster, really wanted was to be a doctor. Every day he took a mysterious book out of his desk and read it while the children were writing. He kept the book locked up, and every child in the school wanted to know what it was.

One day, as Becky Thatcher was passing the teacher's desk, she noticed that the key was in the lock. She looked round. There was nobody in the room. The next moment, the book was in her hands. The name of the book, *Professor Gray's Anatomy*, didn't mean anything to her, so she began to turn the pages. She came at once to a picture. At that moment, Tom Sawyer stepped in at the door. Becky tried to close the book very quickly before he could see the picture, but in her hurry she accidentally tore the page. She pushed the book into the desk and turned the key. She was crying.

"Tom Sawyer, I hate you. I know you're going to tell. And then I'll be punished. I've never been punished in school. I hate you, hate you, hate you!" And she ran out of the room.

"What funny things girls are!" Tom thought. "Never been punished in school! What's a beating? Well, of course I'm not going to tell old Dobbins. But that doesn't help her. Old Dobbins will ask who tore his book. Nobody'll answer. Then he'll do what he always does – ask first one and then another, and when he comes to the right girl, he'll know it without being told. Girls' faces always tell. She'll get punished. That's bad luck for Becky Thatcher."

When the master came and school started, Tom wasn't really interested in his studying. Every time he looked across at the girls' side of the room, Becky's face troubled him.

A whole hour passed. Then Mr Dobbins unlocked his desk and brought out his book. Two of the children watched him anxiously. He opened the book.

When the master stood up and looked at the school, everyone felt fear – even those who knew nothing about the cause of his anger.

"Who tore this book?"

There was not a sound. The master looked at face after face. Then:

"Benjamin Rogers, did you tear this book?"

No.

"Joseph Harper, did you?"

No.

The master looked closely at the faces of all the boys. Then he turned to the girls.

"Amy Lawrence?"

No.

"Gracie Miller?"

No.

"Susan Harper, did you do this?"

No.

The next girl was Becky Thatcher.

"Rebecca Thatcher" – (Tom looked at her face; it was white with terror) – "did you tear – no, look at me – did you tear this book?"

Tom stood up and shouted, "I did it!"

The school couldn't understand this madness. Tom was surprised himself. But when he went to the front of the class to take his punishment, the surprise, the thanks,

Tom says that he tore the book

even the love that shone on him out of poor Becky's eyes seemed enough to pay for a hundred beatings.

Tom was so pleased with his own splendid act that he received his beating – the most cruel that even Mr Dobbins had ever given anyone – without a sound. He didn't even mind the added cruelty of an order to stay in the school for two hours after the other children had gone. He knew who would wait for him outside until the time was over.

That night, he fell asleep with Becky's words still in his ears: "Oh, Tom, how *could* you be so fine!"

Chapter 10
The trial

At last the murder trial began in the court, and the sleepy village woke up. It was the one subject of village talk. Tom couldn't get away from it. He was worried all the time. At last he took Huck to one of his secret places to have a talk.

"Huck, have you ever told anybody about – about that?"

"Of course I haven't. Why do you ask?"

"Well, I was afraid."

"Listen, Tom Sawyer. We wouldn't stay alive for two days if that got found out."

The boys did what they had often done before – went to the barred prison window and gave Muff Potter some smokes and talked to him. He thanked them so many times that they were more troubled than ever. They felt terrible when he said, "You've been really kind to me, boys – better than anybody else in this town. I know that, and I don't forget it. I often say to myself, 'I used to mend all the boys' things, and show them the best places to fish, and help them when I could. And now they've all forgotten old Muff when he's in trouble. But Tom doesn't, and Huck doesn't – they don't forget him,' I say to myself, 'and I don't forget *them*!' Well, boys, I did a terrible thing. I was drunk and mad at the time. That's the only explanation I can think of. But I did it, and now they'll hang me for it – and quite right, too. But what I want to say is, don't *you* ever get drunk, boys, and then you won't ever get here."

Tom went home miserable. Huck felt the same.

The news from the courtroom was bad. At the end of

the second day of the trial, the village was sure: Injun Joe's evidence was clear, and the defence lawyer hadn't been able to shake it.

Tom was out late that night, and came to bed through the window. It was hours before he got to sleep.

All the village went to the courthouse the next day. Potter, pale, frightened, and hopeless, was brought in in chains. All eyes were on him.

Injun Joe was there, his face showing nothing.

The judge arrived.

A witness was called, and he told the court how he saw Muff washing in a stream early in the morning of the day after the murder. The lawyer speaking for the state asked a few more questions and then turned to the defence·lawyer: "Your witness."

"I have no questions to ask this witness."

The next witness spoke about how the knife was found near the body.

"Your witness."

Again the defence lawyer said, "I have no questions to ask this witness."

A third witness said that he had often seen the knife before. It was Potter's own knife.

"Your witness."

"No questions."

The faces of the people in court began to look annoyed. "Is this lawyer going to throw his man's life away without trying to save him?" they wondered.

Other witnesses appeared and were treated in the same way.

At last the defence lawyer rose.

"Your honour," he said to the judge, "at the beginning of this trial I said that we were going to show that the prisoner did this terrible thing, but that he did not know what he was doing – that it was the result of drink and not of evil purpose. I have changed my mind. I am not going to offer that explanation." He turned to the court officer and said: "Call Thomas Sawyer."

Every face in the court, including Potter's, showed surprise and wonder.

Tom took his place in the witness box. He looked very frightened.

"Thomas Sawyer," said the defence lawyer, "where were you on the seventeenth of June about the hour of midnight?"

Tom's eyes went to Injun Joe's face, and he couldn't speak at first. But after a few moments he was able to answer, "In the graveyard."

"A little louder, please. Don't be afraid. You were——"

"In the graveyard."

Injun Joe's smile showed that he didn't think this witness was important.

The lawyer for the defence went on, "Were you anywhere near Horse Williams's grave?"

"Yes, sir."

"Speak just a little louder. How near were you?"

"As near as I am to you now, sir."

"Were you hidden or not?"

"I was hidden."

"Where?"

"Behind the trees right at the edge of the grave."

Injun Joe made a very small movement of surprise.

"Was anyone with you?"

"Yes, sir. I——"

"Wait a moment. You needn't tell us the name yet. We'll call that witness at the right time. Did you carry anything there with you?"

Tom didn't answer at once. He looked uncertain.

"Don't be afraid, my boy. There is no harm in the truth. What did you take there?"

"Only a – a – dead cat."

There were some sounds of laughter. The judge quickly stopped them.

"The defence will bring the remains of that cat to show to the court. Now, my boy, tell us everything that happened. Tell it in your own way. Don't miss out anything, and don't be afraid."

Tom began. At first the words didn't come easily. But slowly, as he described the actions that were so clear in his own memory, he made the people in the court see them too. There was soon no sound except the boy's voice. Every eye was on him as he drew near the end of his story: "And as the doctor swung the board round and Muff Potter fell, Injun Joe jumped with the knife and——"

Crash! Suddenly and very quickly, Injun Joe sprang towards a window, fought free of arms that tried to stop him, and was gone.

Chapter 11
Hidden treasure

Tom was a hero in the village. His days were proud days, but his nights were times of great fear. Injun Joe made his dreams terrible, and he went out at night – if he had to do so – in a state of endless fright.

Huck was the same. Injun Joe's escape had saved him from being a witness at the trial, but Tom had told the whole story to the defence lawyer the night before the great day of the trial, and both boys were afraid. The lawyer had promised to keep their secret, but could Huck be sure? Pity for Muff Potter had made the boys themselves break their solemn promise to say nothing. But Injun Joe was still free – and a terrible danger.

It was quite a long time before adventure called again.

But there comes a time in every healthy boy's life when he *must* go somewhere and dig for hidden treasure. This need suddenly struck Tom one day. He went out to look for Joe Harper – without success. Next he tried to find Ben Rogers – he had gone fishing. At last he met Huck Finn the Red-handed. Huck was always willing to join in anything that was exciting and didn't cost money.

"Where are we going to dig?" he wanted to know.

Tom thought. "Almost anywhere," he said. "Let's try the haunted house. There's sure to be treasure there."

"I don't like ghosts and spirits and things," said Huck.

"But, Huck, ghosts only move around at night. They won't stop us digging in the daytime."

Huck had to agree. So they got two very old spades, and on Saturday afternoon they set out for the haunted house. Nobody had lived there for a very long time. It looked so sad, and there was such silence that the boys were afraid to go in at first. Then they went slowly to the door and looked in. They saw a room without a floor. A few weeds were growing inside. There was no glass in any of the windows, the stairs were broken and dangerous, and the old fireplace was useless. With their hearts beating fast, the two boys went in. They spoke in whispers, and they were ready to run out if they heard a sound.

After a time, they grew less afraid, and they began to look around, rather proud to find themselves so brave. They wanted to look upstairs. It seemed a dangerous thing to do, but curiosity won. They threw their spades into a corner among some weeds, and climbed carefully.

There was nothing upstairs, and they were ready to go down and begin digging ——

"*Sh!*" said Tom.

"What is it?" whispered Huck, white with fear.

"*Sh!* There! Hear it?"

"Yes! Oh! Let's run!"

"Keep still! Don't move! They're coming straight to the door."

The boys lay on the floor, looking through holes in the wood, very frightened.

Two men came into the haunted house. Each boy said to himself, "That's the old Spaniard that people have seen in the village a few times – the 'deaf and dumb Spaniard', as people call him, because he can't hear or speak. I never saw the other man before."

The "other man" was dirty and very poor-looking. The Spaniard was wearing a big Mexican hat and had a lot of white hair and a thick white beard under it. His eyes were hidden by green glasses. When they came in, the "other man" was talking in a low voice. The two men sat down on the ground, facing the door, with their backs to the wall, and the speaker went on. "No," he said. "I don't like it. It's dangerous."

"Dangerous!" The voice of the "deaf and dumb" man who "couldn't hear or speak" sounded angry. It filled the boys with fear: it was the voice of Injun Joe! "Why can't you be a little less afraid? It's not more dangerous than the job we did together up the river."

There was silence for a minute, and then Injun Joe spoke again: "All right. You go back up the river to your own town, and wait there. I'm not afraid to go once more into this town to make a plan for the 'dangerous' job – as you call it. Just now we must decide what to do with the stuff we hid here. It isn't a good place for it."

He went across to the fireplace and pulled up one of the stones under it. A hole appeared, and he took a bag from it. He took about twenty dollars from it for himself and the same amount for the other man. Then he looked around.

"I'll bury it deep in that corner," he said. And he began to dig a hole with his big knife.

The boys watched. They forgot their fear as they thought, "This is the best kind of treasure hunting. Now we don't have to guess where to dig."

Injun Joe's knife struck something.

"Hullo!" he said.

"What is it?" said his friend.

"Bit of wood – no, it's a box, I think. Ah! I've broken a hole in the top."

He put his hand in through the hole and brought something out.

"It's money!"

The two men looked at the handful of coins. They were gold.

Injun Joe's friend said, "We'll soon get the box up. I saw two spades among the weeds in that other corner." He ran and got the boys' spades. Injun Joe took one of the spades, looked at it, shook his head in doubt, said something to himself, and then began to dig with it.

The men soon got the box up and opened it.

"There's thousands of dollars here," cried Injun Joe.

"I heard that Murrel's gang worked round here one summer," said his friend.

"Yes," said Injun Joe, "and this looks like their stuff. I wonder why they left it here."

"Well, you won't need to do that dangerous job here now."

Injun Joe looked angry. "You don't know me," he said. "Or you don't know everything about the job. It's not just taking money. It's revenge!" There was cruelty in his voice. "I'll need your help. When it's done, we'll go to Texas. Go home now, and wait till you hear from me."

"All right. What'll we do with this? Bury it again?"

"Yes. [*Delight in the two boys above.*] No! No! [*Sorrow above.*] I nearly forgot. That spade had fresh earth on it. [*The boys were sick with terror at once.*] Why were any spades here? Why with fresh earth on them? Who brought them here, and where are they now? No, we won't bury it again. We'll take it to my hiding place."

"Oh, of course! You mean number one?"

"No. Number two – under the cross. The other place isn't good enough."

"All right. It's nearly dark enough to start."

Injun Joe got up and looked carefully through a

Injun Joe finds the box of gold

window. He said: "Who brought those spades here? Do you think they may be upstairs?" He put his hand on his knife and turned towards the stairs.

The boys couldn't move.

They heard the steps on the old stairs. Then there was a crash of breaking wood, and Injun Joe landed on the ground in the remains of the stairs.

"Now what's the use of that?" said his friend. "In my opinion, the people who threw those spades there had seen us, and thought we were ghosts – and they're probably still running."

Joe swore for a time. Then he agreed that they should spend the time getting ready to go. Soon afterwards, they left the house as night began to fall. They went towards the river with their precious box.

Tom and Huck got up off the floor. They didn't say much. It was hard to get down to the ground, and they were angry with themselves for bringing the spades. If they hadn't done that, Injun Joe would have hidden the treasure there to wait until he had had his "revenge" ——

A thought came to Tom.

"Revenge? You don't think he means *us*, Huck?"

They talked about it on their way back to the village. They decided that possibly Injun Joe meant someone else. And they agreed to watch for the "Spaniard" and follow him to "number two", wherever that was.

Chapter 12
Injun Joe's revenge

There was good news for the boys and girls of St Petersburg on Friday morning. Becky had at last got her mother to name the next day for the picnic that would start the summer holiday.

It was a joyful company that gathered at Judge Thatcher's house the next morning. It was not the custom for older people to spoil picnics by being present. A few teachers – young ladies of eighteen and young gentlemen of twenty-three – from the Sunday school were going, and the children seemed safe with them. They were to go in the old steamboat, and soon the happy crowd were moving down the main street to the landing place. The last thing Mrs Thatcher said to Becky was, "It'll be late when you get back. Perhaps you ought to spend the night with one of the girls who live near the landing place."

"Then I'll stay with Susy Harper, mother."

But on their way to the landing place, Tom said to Becky, "Instead of going to Joe Harper's, let's climb up the hill and stop at Widow Douglas's. She'll have ice cream! And she'll be really glad to have us."

"Oh, that will be fun!" Then Becky thought for a moment. "But what will my mother say?"

"Your mother won't know, and so what's wrong with the idea? I expect she would have told you to go there if she'd thought of it."

The Widow Douglas's great kindness and ice cream won the argument, and they decided to say nothing to anybody about where they would go.

Five kilometres below St Petersburg, the steamboat

stopped at the mouth of a small stream and tied up. The crowd landed, and soon there was shouting and laughing as the children tried all the different ways of getting hot and tired.

The picnic followed, and then a rest under the trees. Then somebody shouted, "Who's ready for the cave?"

Everybody was. They took their candles and started to climb. The mouth of the cave was high up the hillside, an opening shaped like the letter A.

The long string of lighted candles began the journey down the main passageway. This main passageway was not more than three or four metres wide, but the light of all the candles together hardly reached the top, twenty metres above them. Every few steps, other high and narrower passages branched from it on each side. McDougal's Cave was made up of numberless passages that ran into each other and led nowhere. No man "knew" the cave. That was impossible. Most of the young men knew a part of it, and it was not usual to go far outside this known part. Tom Sawyer knew as much of the cave as anyone.

For a kilometre or more they kept together. Then small groups and pairs began to turn into side passages to surprise their friends by appearing where the passages joined again.

After some time, the different groups came back to the mouth of the cave, hot, dirty, covered with candle drippings, and delighted with the success of the day. They were surprised to find that it was already late. The steamboat's bell had been ringing for half an hour, but only the captain worried about the time.

It was Huck's turn to watch for the "Spaniard" and follow him while Tom went to the picnic. Huck didn't expect to see anybody after eleven o'clock at night, but he was taking a last walk through the village when he did hear something. Two men passed him, and one of them seemed to be carrying something. The box? Huck, with no shoes on his feet, made no sound as he followed them.

The men stopped at Widow Douglas's fence. Before he knew that they had stopped, Huck was very close to them – frighteningly close.

"But they won't see me," he thought. "And if they bury the treasure here, it won't be hard to find."

A man spoke in a very low voice – Injun Joe's: "There are lights in the house. She's got people there."

Huck's heart nearly stopped. They hadn't come to bury the treasure. They'd come for the "revenge" job. He wanted to run away, but he remembered that Widow Douglas had been kind to him more than once. Perhaps these men had come to murder her. He heard the other man say, "We'll have to leave without doing the job."

"Leave?" Injun Joe sounded angry. "I tell you again, I don't care about the money – you can have it. But her husband sent me to prison. He's dead, but I'll have my revenge on his widow. She'll pay for what he did. I'm going to mark her – cut her face with my knife. We'll have to wait till the people go and the lights are out. There's no hurry."

Huck was sure that they were going to wait in silence. And silence was very dangerous. He started to move away backwards, hardly breathing – one step – another step – another. It was safe to turn. He turned and walked forwards – still carefully. At last it was safe to run, and he ran down the hill to the old Welsh farmer's house. There he banged on the door.

The heads of the old man and his two strong sons looked out of windows.

Huck hears Injun Joe's plans for revenge

"Who's banging? What do you want?"

"Let me in – quick!" Huck was nearly crying.

"Is that Huckleberry Finn? All right, boys, let him in. Let's see what the trouble is."

Three minutes later, the old man and his sons, carrying guns, started up the hill. Huck went with them to show them the way, but he stopped fifty metres before the place where he had heard the two men. He hid behind a rock while the Welshman and his sons went on.

Suddenly there was a great banging of guns, and then a cry, Huck didn't wait any longer. He ran down the hill as fast as he could.

Just before daylight on Sunday morning, Huck knocked gently on the old Welshman's door.

"Who's there?"

"Please let me in! It's only Huck Finn!"

"It's a name that can open this door at any time. Come in, boy. And welcome!"

They were strange words to Huckleberry Finn's ears. He couldn't remember ever being "welcome" before.

"Breakfast's nearly ready," said the old man. "I'll tell you what happened. You showed us where to go, so we went as quietly as we could. But then I stood on a dry stick, and we heard them running away. We used our guns, but we don't think any of our bullets hit them. They fired twice at us, but their bullets missed us. When we couldn't hear them any more, we went down and woke the sheriff. He got a number of men together, and they've gone to guard the widow and watch the river bank. As soon as it's light, they're going to search the forest. My boys are with them." He looked closely at Huck. "You look really ill, boy. There's a bed for you after breakfast."

Chapter 13
Lost in the cave

The story of the happenings near the widow's house went quickly round the village. Everybody was early at church, and the news was discussed before the doors opened.

After church, Judge Thatcher's wife spoke to Mrs Harper: "Is my Becky going to sleep all day? I just expected she'd be tired after the picnic."

"Your Becky?"

"Yes." Mrs Thatcher looked surprised. "Didn't she spend the night with you?"

"No."

Mrs Thatcher's face went pale, and she was going to say something when Aunt Polly came up to them.

"Good morning, Mrs Thatcher. Good morning, Mrs Harper. I'll have to speak to Tom about not telling me what he was doing. I suppose he stayed at one of your houses last night."

Mrs Thatcher's face was white now.

"He didn't stay with us," said Mrs Harper. "Joe, have you seen Tom Sawyer this morning?"

"No, Mother."

Anxiety spread quickly. There were worried questions for the children and the young teachers. They all said they hadn't noticed whether Tom and Becky were on board the steamboat on the way home. It had been dark. Nobody had tried to make sure that everybody was there. At last one young man said he was afraid they were still in the cave.

The thieves were forgotten. The steamboat was made ready, and in less than half an hour more than two hundred men were hurrying towards the cave.

All the long afternoon, the village seemed empty and dead. All night the women waited for news. When morning came, the only message from the cave was: "Send more candles, and send food." Mrs Thatcher and Aunt Polly were sick with worry.

The old Welshman came home, covered with candle drippings and very tired. He found Huck still in the bed that he had gone to after eating hardly any breakfast the day before. The boy was very ill with fever.

The St Petersburg doctors were all at the cave, so Widow Douglas came to look after Huck.

Three days and nights passed, and there was still no news from the cave. Sorrow began to rule in the village.

Chapter 14
Tom finds a way out

We must go back to Tom and Becky's part in the picnic. They went happily along the passages with the rest of the children, visiting all the well-known wonders of the cave: The Hall, The Great Church, Aladdin's Palace, and others. Then they joined in the fun in and out of the side passages. After that, they wandered down one of the passages, holding their candles up and reading the names, dates, addresses, and other things written in candle smoke and all mixed together. Still moving along and talking, they hardly noticed that they were now in a part of the cave that had no writing on the walls.

At last Becky said, "Tom, I didn't notice, but it seems a long time since I heard any of the others."

"You're right, Becky. We must start back."

They started along a passage, and went in silence for a long way, looking into each opening. But all the openings were strange. Every time Tom examined a new passage, Becky watched his face, hoping to see him show that he knew it. And he always said, "Oh, it's all right. This isn't the one, but we'll come to it. Don't worry, Becky."

At last Tom had to tell her that he couldn't find the way forward or back.

"Tom, Tom, we're lost! We're lost! We'll never, never get out of this terrible place. Oh, why did we ever leave the others?"

After a time, Tom took Becky's candle and blew it out. No words were needed. Becky understood: they had to save their candles. She knew that Tom had a whole candle and three or four pieces in his pocket, but they had to use them carefully. She began to lose all hope.

At last Becky couldn't go any farther. She sat down. Tom sat with her, and they talked about home, and the friends there, and the comfortable beds, and – most of all – the light. After a time, Becky fell asleep. When she woke, Tom said, "I'm glad you slept, Becky. You'll feel rested now, and we'll find the way out."

A long time after that, Tom said they must go quietly and listen for water. They must find a spring. They found one in the end, and Tom said it was time to rest again.

When Becky wanted to go on, Tom was silent for a moment. Then he said, "Becky, can you bear it if I tell you something? I'm afraid we must stay here, where there's water to drink. This little piece is our last candle. We must wait till they find us."

Becky cried, but at last she said, "When will they miss us, Tom?"

"When they get back to the boat, I expect."

"Tom, it might be dark then. Would they notice we weren't there?"

"I don't know, but of course your mother will miss you as soon as they arrive."

The look on Becky's face told Tom that he had made a bad mistake. It could be a long time before Mrs Thatcher discovered that Becky was not at Mrs Harper's. They sat and watched as the last bit of candle burnt down and went out. They were in darkness.

Sleep came to them while Becky was crying in Tom's arms.

It seemed a very long time before either of them spoke. And then it was Tom who said, "Sh! Did you hear that?"

They both stopped breathing and listened. There was a

sound like a very far distant shout. Tom answered it at once. Then, leading Becky by the hand, he started feeling his way down the passage towards it. After a time, he listened again. Again they heard the sound, and it seemed a little nearer.

"It's them!" said Tom. "They're coming! Come along, Becky. We're all right now!"

They were full of joy. But they had to move slowly. The floor of the passage was uneven. It wasn't long before they came to a deep hole or drop, and had to stop. Tom couldn't find the bottom. He shouted again and again, but the distant shouts were getting farther away. After a few minutes, they had gone altogether. Tom talked hopefully to Becky, but they heard nothing else, and at last they felt their way back to the spring.

Time passed slowly – and now, because they were so hungry, painfully.

There were some side passages near the spring, and Tom decided to explore them. He had a fishing line in his pocket – about sixty metres. He fastened one end to a rock point beside the spring, and he started along the nearest side passage. Becky said she would wait. She was very weak now, and couldn't find the strength to go with him.

Tom felt his way along carefully, letting out the fishing line as he went. At the end of about fifteen metres the passage floor ended in a drop. Tom lay down and felt below, and then as far round the corner as he could reach – nothing. He stretched a little farther to the right, and at that moment, not more than twenty metres away, a hand, holding a handle, appeared from behind a rock!

Tom gave a joyful shout, and immediately the hand was followed by the body it belonged to – Injun Joe's!

Tom couldn't move. He was very glad when he saw

the "Spaniard" turn quickly and move out of sight as fast as he could.

"Why didn't Joe come and kill me for giving evidence in court?" Tom asked himself. He decided that the cave walls had changed the sound of his voice. But his fright made him very weak. "If I can get back to the spring, I'll stay there," he thought. "I daren't take the chance of meeting Injun Joe again."

He was careful not to tell Becky what he had seen. "I only shouted for luck," he said.

But hunger and misery are stronger than fear in the end. After a long wait at the spring, Tom decided to explore a passage in the other direction. He went along it to the end of his fishing line. Then he tried another passage, and another. He followed one more passage as far as his line would reach, and he was just going to go back once more to Becky when he thought he saw a suggestion of daylight far away. He dropped his line and felt his way towards the place, pushed his head and shoulders through a small hole – and saw the broad Mississippi rolling by!

Tom finds a way out of the cave

Chapter 15
Back to the cave

Tuesday afternoon came, and Tuesday evening. The village of St Petersburg was still sad. The lost children had not been found.

In the middle of the night, the church bells rang out. In a moment the streets were crowded with excited people shouting, "They're found! They're found!"

A message was sent to the cave to call back the men, who were still searching there. And then Tom had to tell the story again – it grew better with each telling, of course. He told about finding the hole, about getting poor Becky to believe him, and then helping her to reach the place. He described how he pushed his way out of the hole and then helped Becky out; how at last some men came past in a boat; how he shouted to them, and told them about their experience, and how hungry they were. At first they couldn't believe him: "But you're ten kilometres down the river below the valley the cave is in!" Then they rowed the boy and girl to a house, gave them supper, made them rest until two or three hours after dark, and then brought them home.

About two weeks after Tom's escape from the cave, he went to visit Huck. Huck's fever was gone, and he was getting stronger.

Judge Thatcher's house was on Tom's way back, and he stopped there to see Becky. The judge and some friends asked Tom a lot of questions. Then the judge said, "We can't allow anyone else to get lost there, so I had the entrance closed with a big wooden door with iron on the outside. And I've got the keys."

Tom's face turned white.

"What's the matter, boy? Are you ill?"

"No, sir. I'm not ill. – Injun Joe's in the cave!"

The news spread quickly, and several boats full of men started towards McDougal's cave. Tom went with them. When the cave entrance was opened, a terrible sight came to the men's eyes. Injun Joe lay stretched on the ground, dead. His face was close to the edge of the door, and he had broken his knife, trying to cut his way out.

A few days later, Tom went to see Huck again.

"Huck," said Tom, "we'll have to do something about the money."

"What! Tom, you haven't found out something, have you? Where do you think the money is?"

"Huck, it's in the cave! The money's in the cave!"

"How far into the cave is it, Tom? I've been up and walking for a few days, but I can't walk more than a kilometre, or perhaps two."

"It's about eight kilometres into the cave the way anybody else would go, Huck. But there's a very short way that only I know. I'll take you there in a boat. You needn't even row."

"Let's start now, Tom."

"All right. We want some bread and meat, and a few little bags, candles and some of those new things they call matches, and several fishing lines. We'll use Dan Smith's boat – he's away, and he won't know."

They found Tom's very small entrance, hidden by bushes. Tom tied his first fishing line there, and they went slowly. They passed the spring where Tom and Becky had expected to die. Then, along another passage, Tom stopped. He held up his candle.

"Now look, Huck. Look as far round the corner as you can. Do you see that? There – on the big rock – done with candle smoke."

"Tom, it's a *cross*!"

"Remember, Huck? In the haunted house, Injun Joe said, 'Number two – under the cross.' This is number two. Now we've got to look under the cross."

They climbed down the drop where Tom had been when he saw Injun Joe. Under the cross there were marks that showed them where someone had been digging. Tom began to dig there with his knife. Soon the knife struck wood. It was the box. Tom freed it.

"Let's see if I can lift it," he said.

It weighed about twenty-five kilograms. Tom could lift it, but he couldn't carry it easily.

"I thought so," he said. "I'm glad we brought the little bags."

The money was soon in the bags, and the boys began their journey back to the little hole above the river. There was nobody about, and they were soon in the boat, eating a meal, and waiting for evening.

Tom and Huck dig up the box in the cave

Chapter 16
Widow Douglas's party

It seemed quite late when Tom and Huck took Dan Smith's boat back to its place near the village.

"Now, Huck," said Tom, "we'll hide the money in the roof space above the Welshman's wood store, and I'll come up in the morning, and we'll count and divide. Then we'll find a place out in the forest where it will be safe. Just lie quietly here and watch the bags while I run and get Benny Taylor's little handcart."

He disappeared, and came back with the cart. The bags of money were soon on the cart, covered with some old pieces of cloth, and Tom started, pulling the handcart behind him.

When the boys reached the Welshman's fence, they stopped to rest. They were just going to move on towards the wood store when Mr Jones, the Welshman, came out of his house.

"Hullo!" he said. "Who's that?"

"Huck and Tom Sawyer."

"Good. Come along with me, boys. Everybody's waiting." And he took the handcart and led them to Widow Douglas's house. He left the handcart at the door and pushed Huck and Tom into the widow's sitting room. Everybody important was there: the Thatchers, the Harpers, the Rogerses, Aunt Polly with Sid and Mary, the minister, and a number of others, all wearing their best clothes. The widow received the two boys very kindly. It didn't seem to matter to her that they were covered with dirt from the cave and candle drippings. But Aunt Polly's face was very red as she looked at Tom's clothes.

"Come with me," the widow said. And she led the boys to a bedroom and said, "Now wash, and dress yourselves. Here are two new suits of clothes – shirts, everything. They're Huck's – no, don't thank me, Huck – Mr Jones bought one and I bought the other. But they'll fit both of you. Get into them. We'll wait. Come down when you're ready."

Then she left the room.

Huck said, "Tom, we can get away if we can find a rope. The window isn't very high up."

"Why do you want to get away?"

"I can't go into a crowd like that, Tom. I'm not going down there."

"I'll take care of you," said Tom, who had seen all sorts of cakes and ice cream in the sitting room.

Sid appeared.

"What's all this party about, Sid?" Tom asked.

"It's one of the widow's parties that she often has. This time it's for the Welshman and his sons, because they saved her from trouble that night."

"Well, there's not much harm in that," said Tom. And he led the way down. Huck followed, very unwillingly.

After supper, Mr Jones stood up. He thanked Mrs Douglas for the honour she had done him and his sons.

"But there's another person here who did more that night to prevent a terrible crime," the Welshman said. And he told the part that Huckleberry Finn had played that night. The widow spoke, too, about Huck's brave actions.

Huck almost forgot the great discomfort of his new clothes in the greater discomfort of being stared at and thanked by everybody.

The widow said, "I want to give Huck a home here,

and have him well educated. Then, when the time comes, I hope I'll have enough money to start him in a business."

It was then that Tom said, "That part of it won't be necessary. Huck won't need the money. Huck's rich."

Nobody laughed, but that was because they all had good manners. But there was a rather uncomfortable silence.

"I'll just have to show you," Tom said. He ran out, and came back carrying – with difficulty – the bags of money. "There!" he said. "Half of it's Huck's, and half of it's mine!"

Nobody spoke for a moment. Then everyone asked for an explanation. Tom said he would explain, and he did explain. The story was a long one, but full of interest. There was hardly another sound while Tom was telling it.

The money was counted. There was just over twelve thousand dollars. It was more than anybody in the room had ever seen at one time before.

Chapter 17
Huck's new life

Of course there was great excitement in the poor little village of St Petersburg. It was hard to believe that there could be so much money – in real coins. Every "haunted" house in St Petersburg and the villages round it was pulled to pieces and dug up by treasure hunters – not boys, but men.

The Widow Douglas put Huck's money into banks that paid six per cent. And Aunt Polly asked Judge Thatcher to do the same with Tom's. So each of the boys was now rich, with a dollar coming to him for every weekday in the year – half a dollar on Sundays. In those simple days, a dollar and a quarter a week was enough for a boy's housing and food – and clothes – and baths.

Judge Thatcher had a very high opinion of Tom. "No ordinary boy," he said, "would ever have got my daughter out of the cave."

When Becky told her father how Tom had taken her punishment at school, the judge was even more pleased.

"Yes," he said, "Tom told a lie, but it was a splendid lie – a gentleman's lie. I think Tom will be a great lawyer or a great soldier one day. I'll help him to get into the National Military Academy at West Point to be trained as an army officer, and then into the best law school in America."

Being rich, and being looked after by the Widow Douglas caused Huck Finn to enter a new world, and his sufferings in it were almost more than he could bear. The widow's servants kept him clean and well-dressed, combed and brushed. They put him to bed every night in a bed with perfectly clean bedclothes that seemed to him unfriendly. He had to eat with a knife and fork; he had to use cups and plates; he had to learn to read; he had to go to church; he had to talk so properly that talking had no colour or taste for him. The bars and locks of civilisation seemed to be making him a prisoner.

Huck bore his miseries for three weeks, and then he disappeared. The widow hunted for him everywhere for two days. The public were worried; they searched everywhere; they even looked for his body in the river. Early on the third morning, Tom Sawyer went and looked among some old barrels behind the village stores, and in one of the barrels he found the runaway. Huck had slept there. He had just had a breakfast of stolen bits of food. He was unwashed, uncombed, and dressed in the old clothes that he had worn in the days when he was free and happy.

Tom told him the trouble he had caused. "It's making the widow cry all the time," he said. "You really ought to go back to her."

"Don't talk about it, Tom. The widow's kind and I don't want to hurt her. But I can't bear that life. I can't bear the clothes and I can't do the same things at the same times every day. The widow eats by a bell; she goes to bed by a bell; she gets up by a bell. I can't live that way. Can't we go back to being pirates?"

Tom saw his chance.

"Well, no. We can't be pirates any more because everybody knows about it. But we're starting a new gang. We're going to be robbers. But, Huck, we can't let you into the gang if you aren't high class."

"Can't let me in, Tom? Didn't you let me become a pirate?"

"Yes, but that's different. A robber is more high class than a pirate is – usually. In most countries they're really high up – lords and sirs and things."

"Tom, you've always been my friend. You wouldn't shut me out, would you?"

"Huck, I wouldn't want to, and I don't want to. But what would people say? They'd say, 'Mph! Tom Sawyer's Gang! Some low class people in it!' They'd mean you, Huck. You wouldn't like that, and I wouldn't."

Huck was silent for a time. At last he said, "Well, I'll go back to the widow's for a month, and see if I can bear it, if you'll let me belong to the gang, Tom."

"All right, Huck. That's fair. Come along, old fellow, and I'll ask the widow to be a bit less hard on you."

"Will you, Tom? That's good. If she'll be a bit easier on some of the harder things, I'll get through. When are you going to start the gang and be robbers?"

"Oh, at once. We'll get the boys together and have the initiation tonight, perhaps."

"Have what?"

"Have the initiation."

"What's that?"

"It's swearing to stick together, and never tell the gang's secrets, even if you're cut to pieces. And kill anybody that hurts one of the gang."

"That's fine, Tom."

"Yes. And the swearing must be done at midnight, in the most frightening place you can find. A haunted house is best, but they're all torn down now."

"Well, midnight's good, Tom."

"Yes, And you've got to swear over a grave, and write it in blood."

"That's it, Tom! Much better than being pirates! I'll stay with the widow as long as I can, Tom. And if I get famous as a robber, I expect she'll be proud she gave me a home."

Questions

Questions on each chapter

Chapter 1
1 What was Tom doing when Aunt Polly called out ?
2 Did Tom really have a swim, or did he not?
3 Who was Sid?
4 Why were Tom's clothes torn and dirty?

Chapter 2
1 What did Tom have to paint?
2 What was Ben Rogers doing when he came in sight?
3 What two things did Tom get from Aunt Polly's cupboard?
4 Who took Amy Lawrence's place in Tom's heart?

Chapter 3
1 Why did Tom want to be ill?
2 What did Aunt Polly do with the burning wood?
3 What did Tom and Huckleberry Finn talk about?
4 Where did Tom have to sit as part of his punishment?

Chapter 4
1 What was the *Spirit of the Storm*?
2 Why did Tom take off some of his clothes?
3 Where did "Robin Hood" meet "Guy of Gisborne"?
4 What was Huckleberry Finn's dead cat for?

Chapter 5
1 Whose body was in the new grave?
2 Who were the three men who came to the grave?
3 Whose knife was used to kill the doctor?
4 Who killed the doctor?
5 What did the boys mean by "keep mum"?

Chapter 6
1 Why was Aunt Polly sure that Pain-killer was good?
2 Where was Tom putting the Pain-killer every day?
3 What made Peter, the cat, behave madly?
4 Where was Jackson's Island?

Chapter 7
1 What were the people in the boats looking for?
2 How did Tom cross the river to St Petersburg?
3 Who were the two ladies in the sitting room?
4 When did Tom arrive back on the island?

Chapter 8
1 Where did the people see the boys after the church service?
2 Tom's "dream" was really a description of – what?
3 Where did Aunt Polly find out the truth about the "dream"?
4 What was written on Tom's sycamore bark "letter"?

Chapter 9
1 What did Becky tear?
2 Which two children watched Mr Dobbins anxiously?
3 What "fine" thing did Tom do?
4 What happened to him after that?

Chapter 10
1 Where did Tom and Huck go to see Muff Potter?
2 Who did not ask the first witnesses any questions?
3 Who was called as a witness for the defence?
4 Which way did Injun Joe go to escape from the court?

Chapter 11
1 Who were Tom and Huck afraid of?
2 Where did the boys go to dig for treasure?
3 Who was the "deaf and dumb Spaniard"?
4 What was in the box?
5 Why did Injun Joe look at the spade?

Chapter 12
1 Why didn't older people go on the picnic?
2 Why did the children carry candles?
3 Why did the steamboat's bell ring?
4 Why did Injun Joe want to have revenge?
5 Why did Huck go to the Welshman's house?

Chapter 13
1 What did people discuss outside the church?
2 Who asked about Becky?
3 Who went to look for Tom and Becky?
4 What was the matter with Huck?

Chapter 14
1 Why did Tom blow Becky's candle out?
2 Where did Tom decide to wait?
3 Whose hand – and then body – did Tom see?
4 How did Tom find his way back to the spring?
5 What was the "suggestion of daylight"?

Chapter 15
1 Why did the church bells ring?
2 Where was Injun Joe's body?
3 Where was "number two"?
4 What were the little bags for?

Chapter 16
1 What was on the handcart?
2 Where were all the important people?
3 Why did Huck want to find a rope?
4 Who wanted to give Huck a home?

Chapter 17
1 What was Judge Thatcher's opinion of Tom?
2 Where did Tom find Huck?
3 Which is more "high class": a robber or a pirate?
4 Why did Huck agree to go back to the widow's?

Questions on the whole story

These are harder questions. Read the Introduction, and think
hard about the questions before you answer them. Some of
them ask for your opinion, and there is no fixed answer.

1 Tom Sawyer seems to have read quite a lot of books. Can you
  name *three kinds* of stories that he had read?

2 Aunt Polly:
   Do you know someone who is rather like Aunt Polly?
   a In what ways is she like her?
   b In what ways is she different?

3 Aunt Polly believed the old saying: "Spare the rod and spoil the child" (If you don't punish children for faults, you will harm them).
   a Name *two* of the punishments she gave Tom.
   b Do you think she was cruel to him? Give a reason for your answer.

4 The Mississippi:
   a Where does the river start? (Look at a map.)
   b Where does it end?
   c How wide is it near "St Petersburg"?
   d How long did it take the steamboat to cross the river to St Petersburg?

5 Huckleberry Finn:
   Give reasons for your answers to these questions.
   a Do you find him an interesting character?
   b Do you believe that there are still boys like him?
   c At the end of the book, he goes back to Widow Douglas's. Do you think he will stay there?

6 Injun Joe:
   a What do we know about him before the murder of Dr Robinson?
   b How does he die?
   c Are you glad when he dies? Why?

7 Which of the "Adventures" of Tom Sawyer did you read with most pleasure? Why?

8 Do you think any of the boys in this story are like Samuel Clemens (Mark Twain) as a boy? Can you give examples?

9 Why do you think the book has been so successful?

New words

bark
the covering outside the wood of a tree

bury
put under the ground; put a person in a **grave**, a hole in the ground in a **graveyard**

drunkard
a man who always takes a lot of strong drink

evidence
the things that a person (a **witness** who has seen them happen) tells to a court of law

fever
illness that makes a sick person very hot

gang
men who work as a group, often as criminals

ghost
the spirit of a dead person that visits (**haunts**) places it knew when it was alive

log
a thick round part of a tree. Logs from the forest were fastened together to make a flat **raft** to travel down the Mississippi to a port.

marbles
small balls of glass etc. used in children's games

quarterstaff
a long thick stick used for fighting in Robin Hood's time

revenge
harm done to a person in return for harm received from that person

spit
throw out liquid (saliva) from the mouth

steam
water in the form of a gas made by boiling. A **steamboat** is a boat driven by the power of steam.

wart
a small hard growth on a person's skin